Snow White and the Seven Dwarfs

PaRragon

Bath · New York · Cologne · Melbourne · Delhi
Hong Kong · Shenzhen · Singapore

Four steps for enjoyable reading

Traditional stories and fairy tales are a great way to begin reading practice. The stories and characters are familiar and lively. Follow the steps below to help your child become a confident and independent reader:

Once there was a pretty girl called Snow White. She lived in a palace with the queen. The queen was pretty too. But not as pretty as Snow White.

Step 1
Read the story aloud to your child. Run your finger under the words as you read.

Step 2
Look at the pictures and talk about what is happening.

Step 3

Read the simple text on the right-hand page together. When reading, some words come up again and again, such as **the**, **to**, **and**. Your child will quickly get to recognize these high-frequency words by sight.

The queen did not like Snow White.

Step 4

When your child is ready, encourage them to read the simple lines on their own.

Once there was a pretty girl named Snow White. She lived in a palace with the queen. The queen was pretty, too. But not as pretty as Snow White.

The queen did not like
Snow White.

The queen had a magic mirror. Every day she asked it, "Mirror, mirror on the wall, who is the prettiest of all?"

One day, the mirror said, "Snow White is the prettiest."

The queen was very cross. "Take Snow White away," she cried.

The hunter took Snow White
into the woods.

"Run away, Snow White,"
he said.

"Why, what have I done?"
asked Snow White.

"You are too pretty,"
he said. "Run and hide."

Snow White ran away into
the woods.

Soon, Snow White was lost in the woods. It was beginning to get dark when she found a path. She followed the path in the moonlight.

She could see a little house.

The house was dark and there was no one at home. Inside, there were seven little chairs and seven little beds. Snow White felt so tired, she lay down and fell asleep.

When she woke up, she saw seven dwarfs.

"Who are you?" they asked. Snow White told them her story and began to cry.

"You can live here with us!" they said happily.

"Don't be sad," said the seven dwarfs. "We will look after you."

Snow White was happy living with the dwarfs. Every day, the dwarfs went to work.

"Be careful not to talk to strangers," they warned her. "They may not be who they say they are."

Snow White looked after the
dwarfs' little house and their
big garden.

Meanwhile, the wicked queen asked her magic mirror who was the prettiest now. And again the mirror said Snow White. The queen flew into a rage. She poisoned an apple.

The wicked queen visited the little house in the woods. She pretended to be an old woman selling apples. Snow White took the poisoned apple.

Snow White ate the apple and
fell to the ground.

When the dwarfs came home,
they thought Snow White was
dead. They put her in a glass case
and carried it to the top of a hill.

Then the dwarfs sat down and cried.

Before long, a prince rode by.
He stopped when he saw
Snow White.

"Who is she?" he asked. The
dwarfs told him her story.

The prince lifted the lid from the
glass case. Snow White looked so
pretty that the prince kissed her.
Suddenly, Snow White gasped
and spat out the bad apple!

The kiss woke Snow White. She sat up.

The prince took Snow White back to his palace.

"Will you marry me?" he asked.

"I will be very happy to marry you," she said.

And so the dwarfs all went to the wedding. It was a very happy day. But the wicked queen was not invited!

They never saw the wicked
queen again.